THE McELDERRY BOOK OF
Grimms' Fairy Tales

For Mary Attard—S.P.

For Joanna—E.C.C

Margaret K. McElderry Books
An imprint of Simon & Schuster Children's Publishing Division
1230 Avenue of the Americas, New York, New York 10020
Text copyright © 2002 by Saviour Pirotta
Illustrations copyright © 2002 by Emma Chichester Clark
First published in Great Britain in 2002 by Orchard Books, a Division
of Watts Publishing Group Ltd, London
First U.S. edition, 2006
Published by arrangement with Orchard Books, a Division of Watts
Publishing Group Ltd
The text for this book is set in Usherwood Book.
Manufactured in China
10 9 8 7 6 5 4 3 2
CIP data for this book is available from the Library of Congress.
ISBN-13: 978-1-4169-1798-4
ISBN-10: 1-4169-1798-5
0410 CCO

THE McELDERRY BOOK OF
Grimms' Fairy Tales

retold by

Saviour Pirotta

illustrated by

Emma Chichester Clark

Margaret K. McElderry Books

New York   London   Toronto   Sydney

Contents

The Sleeping
The Story of

The king and queen of a faraway country had everything they could possibly want: servants, a palace, two crowns each, and thousands of loyal subjects who loved and respected them. There was only one thing missing in their lives: a son or a daughter to inherit their kingdom.

"How I wish I had a child," sighed the queen one day as she walked alone in the royal gardens.

Just then a frog jumped out in her path, startling her.

"Do not be sad," said the frog. "Before long you will have a child." And he was right. A year later the queen gave birth to a baby girl with rosy cheeks and curly locks of hair.

The king was overjoyed and ordered a great christening feast. He invited all the nobles of the land. He invited the fairies, too, so they would present his daughter with magic gifts.

6

Beauty

Briar Rose

"But we can't invite all thirteen of them," said the queen. "We have only twelve golden dishes."

"We'll have to leave one out, then," said the king.

Preparations for the feast began, and soon the day of the christening arrived. The guests showered the baby princess with gifts: golden lockets and diamond rings; clockwork toys and picture books; even a treasure chest full of pearl necklaces. Then the twelve invited fairies formed a tight ring around her cradle.

"I give you the gift of wisdom," said the first fairy, scattering a shower of golden leaves around the softly sleeping baby.

"I give you beauty," cried the second fairy, waving her arms to fill the air with shooting stars.

"And I give you strength," said the third fairy.

One by one the other fairies stepped forward. "I give you confidence."

"I give you patience."

"Friendliness."

"Health."

"Love."

"Happiness."

"Riches."

"Kindness."

Soon only the twelfth fairy remained to present her gift. She was about to speak when there came a clap of thunder so loud that the very foundations of the palace shook and everyone trembled. Then the uninvited fairy flew into the room. She was dressed entirely in black.

"Good evening, Your Majesties," she rasped in her deep, throaty voice. She leaned over the princess's cradle, her eyes gleaming with malice.

"Please don't hurt her," begged the queen.

"Hurt her?" cooed the wicked fairy. "Oh no, I've come to give the little princess a very special gift."

"The princess has everything she needs already," said the king.

The wicked fairy ignored him. "When the princess is

fifteen years old, she will prick her finger on a spindle—and die."

Everyone in the room gasped. The wicked fairy looked around her in triumph, then disappeared with another clap of thunder.

The twelfth fairy stepped forward. "Your Majesty," she said to the queen, "I still have to give the princess my gift."

"Can you reverse the horrible curse?" asked the queen.

"I'm afraid not," said the fairy. "My magic is simply not strong enough. But I can soften it. The princess will not die when she pricks her finger on the spindle; she will merely fall asleep for one hundred years."

The next day the king ordered all the spinning wheels in the country to be burned. "Our daughter will never prick her finger on a spindle," he promised the queen. "She will never fall asleep for a hundred years."

Time passed and everyone forgot about the wicked fairy's curse. But the other fairies'

gifts were fulfilled: The princess grew up
to be a beautiful and kind girl. Everyone
in the kingdom loved her.

On the morning of her fifteenth
birthday, while the king and queen were
not at home, the princess amused herself
by exploring the parts of the palace she
had never been to before. Soon she
came to a curious tower with a narrow
staircase. At the top of the stairs was a
door, and behind the door a dusty little
room. The princess peeped in, trying to
see beyond the cobwebs.

"Hello, my dear!"

The princess jumped. There was an old
lady sitting in the corner of the room.
She was dressed entirely in black.

"What are you doing?" asked the
startled princess.

"Spinning," said the old lady, twirling
the wheel on a strange machine. "Have
you never seen a spinning wheel before?"

"No," said the princess. And she came

closer to have a better look. The old woman smiled.

"What's that?" asked the princess, pointing to a sharp stick bobbing and turning next to the wheel.

"That's the spindle," said the old woman. "You can touch it if you like."

The princess reached out and touched the spindle. "Ouch," she cried as she pricked herself on the needle and a drop of blood mushroomed on her finger.

"Happy birthday," cackled the old woman, who was, of course, the wicked fairy in disguise.

The princess swayed and fell back on an old couch, at once lost in sleep. Almost instantly, everyone else in the palace fell asleep too: The king and queen, who had just come home, slumped back on their thrones; the cook, who was showing them the princess's birthday cake, dozed off with the cake in his hands. In the kitchen the fire stopped roaring and the spit on which a goose was slowly turning came to a halt. Out in the stables the horses and the stable boys yawned and fell down on the straw. The doves on the rafters tucked their heads under their wings; even the spiders fell asleep in their cobwebs on the palace ceiling. All was still.

Soon a thick hedge of thorny bushes grew around the

12

palace, shutting it off from the world, hiding it from view. Years passed, and the hedge grew into a forest. Many people tried to slash their way through it, hoping to find the palace and the princess rumored to be sleeping within. But no one succeeded; the thorny trees kept everyone out.

Then one day a prince from a foreign country came by on his white charger. He'd heard an old storyteller tell of a beautiful princess who slept in the tower of a lonely palace and he wondered if the legend was true. The prince ventured into the forest, his sword in his hand. The old storyteller had mentioned enormous trees that tore at your clothes with nail-sharp thorns, but the prince saw nothing like that. The trees around him were covered in pink blossoms, not thorns. The hundred years were over, and the wicked fairy's curse was slowly beginning to fade.

Soon the prince reached the palace. How silent and sad it was! All he could hear was the rustling of the wind as it blew long-dead leaves around the courtyard. The guards were asleep at the gate, their helmets covered in a thick layer of dust.

The prince left his horse outside and entered the palace. He saw the king and the queen slumped on their thrones.

He heard their gentle snoring as they slept. *Where is the princess?* he wondered. He began to explore the palace, stepping carefully over the sleeping people and animals. At last he found himself in a little tower room. There was a spinning wheel in the corner, and on the couch lay the princess, still as beautiful as the day she had fallen asleep. She looked so bewitching, so serene, the prince couldn't help himself. He bent down and kissed her on the lips. The princess stirred and opened her eyes.

"You're here, at last," she whispered. The prince looked so handsome and strong that the princess couldn't help herself either. She fell in love with him straight away.

"Have I been asleep for long?" she asked.

"A hundred years," said the prince. "But now it's time for your life to begin again." He helped the princess to her feet and they walked slowly down the narrow stairs, hand in hand. As they moved from room to room, the palace gradually came back to life. The spiders stirred on the palace ceiling, the doves in the rafters cooed and flapped their wings, and the horses and the stable boys rose to their feet. In the kitchen the fire roared back to

life and continued to cook the goose, while the spit started to turn round and round again. In the throne room the cook jumped up with the birthday cake still in his hands.

"Do Your Majesties like the cake?" asked the cook, wondering why on earth the king and queen were yawning and stretching and rubbing the sleep out of their eyes.

"We do indeed," said the queen, who had seen the handsome prince leading the princess into the room. "But I think we shall need a wedding cake too!"

The prince and the princess were married right there and then, and lived happily and contentedly for the rest of their lives.

The Magic
The Story of

Once there was a woodcutter and his family who lived close to a great forest. The woodcutter was very fond of his children, a boy called Hansel and a girl called Gretel, but their stepmother hated them and often used to scold them for no reason at all.

Now, it happened that a famine spread across the land and the woodcutter had no food to give his family.

"What is to become of us?" he said to his wife one night as they were getting ready for bed. "We barely have enough food for ourselves—how can we feed the children?"

"I'll tell you what to do," said his wife. "Tomorrow we'll take Hansel and Gretel deep into the forest. I'll give them a piece of bread each and you can light a fire for them. Then, when they have eaten and fallen asleep,

Gingerbread House
Hansel and Gretel

we'll creep away and leave them behind. They'll never find their way home and we'll be rid of them once and for all."

The woodcutter was horrified. "I couldn't possibly leave my children in the forest," he said. "They might be devoured by hungry animals."

"Well, then," snapped his wife, "you might as well start making our coffins right now." And she went on arguing and cajoling until the woodcutter agreed to do as she said. The poor man went to bed with a great sadness in his heart, for he loved his children very much.

Now, Hansel and Gretel were so hungry, they could not sleep and so they overheard every single word their parents had said. Gretel started crying, but Hansel comforted her and said, "Don't worry. We'll find our way back somehow."

When he was sure the grown-ups were asleep, Hansel crept downstairs to the garden, where the moonlight gleamed on hundreds of little white stones lying in the soil. He filled his pockets with the stones and, quick as a mouse, returned to bed.

Early the next morning, the woodcutter's wife shook the children awake. "Get up, you lazy good-for-nothings," she said. "We're going to the forest to collect wood. Here is a piece of bread each for your lunch. Don't eat it before then, because you won't be getting anything else." Then she locked the front door and all four set off toward the forest.

They had not gone far when Hansel turned to look
back at the house. His father said, "Hansel, what are
you looking at?"

"I thought I saw my cat sitting on the roof,"
said Hansel.

"That's not your cat, you fool," said the woodcutter's
wife. "That's the morning sun shining on the chimney."

They walked deeper into the forest. Every now
and then, Hansel turned to look back at the house,
but he wasn't really trying to see his cat; he was
dropping stones on the forest path to leave a trail
behind him.

21

When they reached the middle of the forest, the woodcutter asked his children to collect a big pile of brushwood. Then he built a fire and when it was roaring away, he settled them down beside it. "Now eat your bread, my little ones," he said. "You deserve a rest. Your stepmother and I are going to chop some wood. When it's time to go home, we'll come back and fetch you."

Hansel and Gretel sat by the fire and ate their lunch. They were not at all scared, for they could hear their father chopping wood nearby. After a while they fell asleep. When they woke up again, it was dark

and the forest echoed with the sound of hooting owls and howling wolves.

Gretel trembled with fear, but Hansel said, "Look, there are my stones shining in the moonlight," and they followed the trail of pebbles all the way back home.

They knocked at the door and their wicked stepmother shouted at them, "What kept you so long, you naughty children? Your father and I were worried about you." But the woodcutter hugged his children close; he was glad they were safe and unharmed.

Food was still scarce, so a short time later the

23

stepmother started to complain again. "There is nothing for it," she said. "We must try to get rid of the children once more."

"No," said the woodcutter, "I shall not let my children go. I missed them too much the last time." But his wife went on arguing and cajoling until she wore him down again, so that he agreed to her wicked plans.

Once again, Hansel and Gretel overheard their parents' argument through the wall. So when the lights were out, Hansel crept downstairs to fetch more stones. But this time his stepmother had locked the door, so he returned to bed with empty pockets.

In the morning the children were given a hunk of bread and led into the forest again. Hansel, not having any stones, left a trail of bread crumbs behind him.

"Hansel," asked his father, "why do you keep stopping all the time?"

"I thought I saw my pigeon on the roof of our house," answered Hansel.

"You silly fool," said his stepmother, "that's not your pigeon—that's the sun shining on the chimney."

They walked and walked until they reached a dark part of the forest they had never seen before. The children helped

their father light a fire, and then their stepmother said, "Rest here, children, your father and I are going to chop some firewood. We'll come and get you in the evening."

Hansel and Gretel sat by the fire and, before long, they fell asleep. They were woken up by the screeching of bats. Night had fallen, the fire had burned out, and the children realized that, once again, their parents had abandoned them in the forest.

"Don't worry, Gretel," said Hansel. "We'll follow the trail of bread crumbs till we're home."

But the birds had eaten up all the bread crumbs and the children were completely lost. All night long they wandered through the forest, holding on to each other for courage. They walked and walked until, at dawn, they spied a white bird in the trees.

"Look at him," said Hansel. "He must have plenty of crumbs to eat, for he sounds very happy."

The bird chirped and flew off. The children followed and soon they came to a little cottage among the trees. What a delicious little house it was! The walls were made of gingerbread, the roof of cake and chocolate, and the windowpanes of spun sugar, run through with twists of lemon and lime.

"Some food at last," said Hansel hungrily. And he tore off a part of the roof, while Gretel broke off a piece of windowpane and started nibbling it. They hadn't had such a delicious treat for ages, and they were munching away happily when a voice inside the cottage said:

"Nibble, nibble like a mouse,

Who is gnawing at my house?"

Hansel and Gretel answered:

"The wind, the wind.

You can only hear the wind."

Then the door of the cottage creaked open and a strange old woman came out. "What lovely little children you are," she cried, peering at them through bleary eyes. "And all alone in the forest too. Come inside, come inside, I'll make you a proper meal."

Hansel and Gretel laid down their sugar and chocolate and followed the old woman into the house. Now, this old woman might have looked harmless, but she was, in fact, a wicked witch who had built the cottage using all things sweet and enticing so she could lure children into it. You see, children were her favorite food, and when she caught some, she would fatten them up and roast them in the oven for her dinner.

She gave Hansel and Gretel some pancakes with roast potatoes, some parsnips with butter and jam, and some hot milk. Then she showed them the heaps of pearls and jewels she had lying around the house. When Hansel and Gretel were tired of playing, she tucked them up to sleep in her comfortable, clean bed. The children thought they were in heaven.

But early next morning the witch dragged Hansel out of bed and locked him in a cage. Then she kicked Gretel awake and said, "Light the fire, child; we're making some porridge to fatten up your brother. When he is nice and plump, I shall roast him and eat him."

Gretel was beside herself with grief when she saw Hansel in the cage, but there was nothing she could do except obey the witch. For the next few weeks Hansel was given all kinds of delicious food to eat, but Gretel had to be content with nothing but crab shells and potato peelings. Every day the witch went up to the cage and said:

"Stretch out a finger, you little brat.

Let's see if my food is making you fat."

Hansel, who knew that the witch could not see very well, would stick a chicken bone through the bars.

"I can't understand why you are still so scrawny," grumbled the witch. "You are eating me out of house and home."

When four weeks had gone by, the witch grew tired of waiting. She said to herself: "It's my birthday tomorrow; I shall eat both children at once and have myself a feast."

Early the next morning she made Gretel fetch the water while she fired and stoked the oven. When Gretel returned from the brook, she said, "Check the oven, girl—see if it is hot enough to bake bread."

"How do I check it?" asked Gretel.

"You silly child," cried the witch. "You creep in and have a good look round."

Aha, thought Gretel, *she means to lock me in the oven and cook me.* So she said, "But how do I get in?"

"For goodness' sake," snapped the witch. "You climb in like this." And she got down on all fours and stuck her head in the oven. Gretel gave the witch a mighty push and the witch tumbled headfirst into the fire.

"You wicked child!" cried the witch.

Gretel slammed the oven door shut and drew the bolt. The witch howled and screamed but it was all in vain: Gretel would not open the door. Soon the witch stopped

31

shouting and knocking because her goose was well and truly cooked.

Gretel set her brother free and the two of them hugged and danced around the place for joy. Then they filled their pockets with pearls and jewels from the witch's treasure and set off to try and find their way home.

Soon they came to a stream where there was no bridge or raft to take them across. Gretel saw a duck and sang:

"Dear duck as white as snow,

Across the river we shall go."

The duck came to them, quacking. She let Hansel on her back and took him across the river. Then she carried Gretel, and when both children were safely on the other side of the water, she returned to her nest in the reeds and sat on her eggs.

Hansel and Gretel walked and walked for hours until they came to a part of the forest that seemed familiar to them. Then Gretel said, "Look, Hansel. There's our house in the distance."

And Hansel said, "Look, there's my cat on the roof and my pigeon on the chimney."

So they ran home and found their father sitting at

the kitchen table. His wife had died, and he was all alone. The poor woodcutter had not known a happy moment since he had left his beloved children in the forest. Hansel and Gretel ran to him and hugged and kissed him. Then they emptied out their pockets until the table was covered in pearls and jewels.

"We shall never be poor or hungry again," said Gretel, and the three of them lived together in perfect happiness.

The Magic Bear and
The Story of Snow

A poor woman had two rose trees growing outside her cottage, one with beautiful white blooms and the other with red. She also had twin girls, whom she had named after the rose trees. Both girls were happy and beautiful, but, like the rose trees, they were quite different from each other. Rose Red liked nothing better than to run wild in the meadows, picking flowers and chasing butterflies. Snow White, on the other hand, preferred to stay at home, reading or helping her mother with the household chores.

Every night, after the supper dishes had been washed, the girls would listen to their mother reading a story. They would sit on little cushions and work at their embroidery, while Rose Red's pet dove preened itself on a perch and Snow White's pet lamb snuggled close to the fire.

34

the Handsome Prince
White and Rose Red

One winter's night, while Mother was halfway through a fairy tale, there was a loud knock at the door and someone shouted, "Is anyone in?"

"Open up, children," said the mother. "It might be a lost traveler looking for shelter."

Rose Red opened the door, and an enormous brown bear stuck his snout inside the warm cottage. Rose Red screamed and leaped back, while Snow White dived under the table. The lamb bleated in alarm and the dove put its head under a wing.

"Don't be afraid of me," said the bear. "I mean you no harm. It's freezing out here and I just want to warm my paws by the fire."

"Rose Red, let Mr. Bear in," said Mother. "Snow White, come out from under that table."

So the bear came in and sat by the fire. Mother continued the story, and pretty soon the girls grew bold and leaned against the bear for comfort. The lamb, too, came close and snuggled up to him, while the dove pulled its head out from under its wing and went on preening its feathers.

At the end of the story the bear asked the girls to brush his coat. They fetched a broom and swept his back until his fur was sleek and smooth. Then they went to bed, while their new friend stretched out and went to sleep by the fire.

In the morning the girls let the bear out and he wandered off into the snow. But that evening he returned to hear more stories and to sleep at the hearth. And so it continued till the spring came and the snow

in the forest began to melt. Then the bear said, "I shall
not return tonight. I must go to the mountains, where
I have to guard my treasure from the dwarves. In winter,
when the ground is frozen, they cannot dig it up, but in
spring, when the ground is soft, they manage to dig
through and steal my gold."

Snow White and Rose Red were quite sad when they
heard that the bear would not be visiting any longer, for
they had grown very fond of him. Snow White opened
the door, and as the bear passed through, the bolt
snagged him on the hip and pulled off a chunk of his
soft fur. Rose Red thought she saw a flash of gold
underneath, but she wasn't sure, and she did not say
anything about it. The bear ran off across the snow
and was soon lost to sight.

A few days later Snow White and Rose Red went into the forest to collect some firewood. There they found a fallen tree lying across the path. Behind it something was jumping up and down like a giant grasshopper. When they got nearer, they saw it was a dwarf with his long beard trapped under the tree trunk.

"How did you manage to get trapped so, good sir?" asked Rose Red.

"If you must know, you meddling creatures, I was chopping some wood to cook my dinner," snarled the dwarf. "There's nothing wrong with that, is there? Now come on, don't just stand there, help me pull my beard out."

The girls tugged at the beard with all their strength, but it was no use; the poor dwarf seemed well and truly stuck. So Snow White whipped out a pair of scissors and— *snip, snip*—she cut off the tip of his beard.

"What did you do that for?" screamed the dwarf. "How can I go about with the tip of my beard missing? You silly, insolent creatures, don't meddle with me or I'll put a curse on you." And without as much as a "thank you for freeing me," he pulled a bag of gold out of the hollow tree trunk and disappeared with it into the forest.

The girls hoped they would never run into the ungrateful dwarf again, but barely a week had passed when they met him once more by a brook. The girls had gone there to catch a fish for their supper and, as they approached the water, they saw something leaping about in the reeds. At first they thought it was a giant frog, but then, as they got closer, they realized it was the rude dwarf.

"Good morning," said Red Rose. "And what is the matter with you today?"

"Can't you see?" snapped the dwarf. "My blessed beard has gotten tangled in my fishing line and a big fish is about to pull me into the water. Help me, will you? Don't just stand there, watching me drown."

The girls tried very hard to disentangle the dwarf from the tackle, but the fish kept pulling the line out of their hands. So, once again, Snow White produced her sewing scissors and—*snip, snip*—she cut off a good portion of the dwarf's beard.

"Are you mad?" howled the dwarf the moment he was free. "Can't you see that you have disfigured my face completely? I'll never be able to show my face outside the house again. But I'll pay you back, you insolent hussies, never fear." And with that he fished a bag of pearls out from among the reeds and disappeared down the road.

A week later the girls' mother sent them to buy ribbons at the market. Their way lay across the heath, and as they walked past a huge rock, they saw an enormous eagle wheeling overhead. The eagle landed behind the rock and a moment later the girls heard someone howling in agony. They ran round the rock, and what did they find? The eagle had snatched their old friend the dwarf by the seat of his trousers and was trying to lift him off the ground.

"Get over here and help me, will you?" cried the dwarf. "Can't you see this monster is about to have me for its breakfast?"

At once, the girls grabbed the dwarf by his coattails and tried to pull him free from the eagle's claws. The eagle pulled too, but its claws were no match for the strong girls. At last it let go of the dwarf and flew off into the sky.

"You clumsy creatures," said the dwarf to the girls as he rubbed his bottom. "Couldn't you have been a bit more careful with my coat? Look, it's torn to shreds. Now I'll have to spend money on another one." Then he pried a bag of diamonds out from under the rock and was gone.

On their way home from the market, the girls chanced upon the dwarf a fourth time. He was sitting on the grass with his diamonds scattered in piles around him. The evening sun shone on the precious stones and made them shimmer and sparkle. The girls, who had never seen a precious stone close up before, couldn't help staring.

"What are you gawping at?" shouted the dwarf, who had not been expecting anyone out on the heath so late. "Have you never seen diamonds before, or are you planning to kill me and rob me? Be off with you, you vandals, you robbers, you thieves—" He was still raging and howling when a bear leaped out of the trees and pounced on him. The dwarf's attitude changed right away. "Please, dear bear," he begged, "do not harm me. I'll give you all my treasure. Eat those girls instead of me. They're much bigger than I am and their flesh is not so tough."

But the bear ignored his pleas; he raised his enormous paw and—*thwack*—dealt him a mighty blow. The dwarf fell limp on the ground.

The girls screamed and started running away. But the bear called out to them and said, "Snow White, Rose Red, wait for me."

Then the girls recognized their old friend and stopped running. They waited for him to catch up with them and, as he approached, his fur melted away and he was transformed into a handsome prince.

"I am a king's son," he said. "That wicked dwarf stole my treasure and put a spell on me, so that I was forced to live as a bear until he was slain. Now I am free to go home."

Some time later Snow White married the prince and Rose Red his brother. The girls' mother came to live with them in the palace and she brought her two rose trees with her. Every year they continued to bear the most beautiful blooms: snow white and rose red.

The Golden-Haired

The Story

Once there was a woman who was expecting a baby. She and her husband had spent many years wishing and praying for a child, and now at last their wish was coming true.

They lived in a small cottage next to a beautiful garden. This place belonged to a wicked witch and was surrounded by a high wall so that no one dared to go in.

One day the woman looked out her back window and saw a bed of rapunzel growing in the witch's garden. It looked so fresh and wholesome that the woman could think of nothing else but eating a big bowl of it. Her husband was beside himself with worry, for she refused to touch anything else and became quite pale and drawn. One night the poor woman said, "Husband,

Girl in the Tower

of Rapunzel

if I do not have some rapunzel soon, I believe I shall die and take my child with me."

Then her husband, who loved her very much, said to himself, "I'd rather risk my own life than hers and my child's." And so that night he climbed over the garden wall and stole some rapunzel from the witch.

His wife promptly made a salad with it and ate it. But no sooner had she finished eating than she looked out the window again and said, "I believe I shall touch nothing else for the rest of my life but rapunzel."

The husband had no choice but to creep into the witch's garden once again and get some more of the herb. This time he was not so lucky. The witch was lying in wait behind a tree, and the moment he stepped into her garden, she grabbed him by the arm.

"How dare you steal my rapunzel?" she growled, the hairs on her chin bristling with rage.

"Forgive me, I beg you," said the husband. "The herb is not for me but for my sick wife who is expecting a child. She longs so much for your rapunzel that I fear she might die if I do not take her some."

"In that case," said the witch, "you can have as much of the herb as you want. But only on one condition: When your child is born, you must give it to me. I shall not harm it but will look after the baby as if it were my own flesh and blood."

The husband was terrified of the witch and agreed to give her the child. Then he returned home and gave his wife the rapunzel.

A few months later the baby was born. It was a girl, and as soon as she uttered her first cry, the witch appeared. The parents begged her in vain to let them keep their daughter, but the witch picked up the child, called her Rapunzel, and took her away.

Rapunzel grew up to be a beautiful girl. She had eyes the color of jade and long hair that shone like spun gold. When Rapunzel was twelve years old, the witch locked her up in a tower, deep in the middle of a thick forest.

It was a bare and hateful place, with no stairs or door but just a small window in the little room at the top. When the witch wanted to come in, she would stand at the foot of the tower and say:

"Rapunzel, Rapunzel,

Sweet and fair,

I am here,

Let down your hair."

Then Rapunzel would lean out of the window so her long tresses would tumble down to the ground. The witch would grab Rapunzel's locks and very slowly climb up to the window. Rapunzel, of course, could never get out of the tower; she was trapped in it for good, with not a single soul for company.

Now, one day a prince was riding through the forest on his horse. He heard Rapunzel singing and her sweet voice cast a spell over him. He tried in vain to find a way into the tower, but there was no door, no ladder—just smooth, slippery stone. *There must be a way in and out of this place,* thought the prince. *I shall hide nearby until someone comes.* In the evening the witch appeared with some food for Rapunzel. She stood at the foot of the tower and called:

> *"Rapunzel, Rapunzel,*
> *Sweet and fair,*
> *I am here,*
> *Let down your hair."*

Rapunzel leaned out of the window. When the prince saw her, he could not take his eyes away from her. Oh, how beautiful she was: those jade green eyes, those rosy cheeks, that long golden hair. The prince was enchanted.

When the witch had left, the prince stood under the tower and, with his heart beating wildly in his chest, called:

> *"Rapunzel, Rapunzel,*
> *Sweet and fair,*
> *I am here,*
> *Let down your hair."*

Down tumbled the golden tresses, and up climbed the prince. What a shock Rapunzel had! She had never seen an ordinary man before, let alone a king's son in all his finery. But then the prince started to talk to her and his gentle voice soothed away her fears.

"Come away with me," he said. "I shall love you and make you my queen."

"But how can I get out of this accursed tower?" said Rapunzel, who had also fallen in love with the prince.

"Do not fret," said the prince. "I will find a way."

And he did. Every night the prince brought Rapunzel a skein of silk, with which she wove a long ladder. This she kept hidden from the witch in a chest. When the ladder was nearly finished, the prince said, "I have built a palace for you—it is the most beautiful home in the world, and you will be happy there."

"I can't wait to see it," said Rapunzel. But that very same night she made a terrible mistake; she said to the witch, "How is it that you take so long to climb up my hair? My prince is with me in a moment."

"What is this I hear, you deceitful child?" roared the witch. "I shut you off from the rest of the world and you have betrayed me!" In a fit of rage she seized a pair of scissors and viciously lopped off Rapunzel's hair. Then she grabbed her by the ears and, chanting a magic spell, cast her into a thorny desert. That night she returned to the tower and fastened Rapunzel's chopped-off tresses to a hook by the window.

Shortly after midnight the prince arrived. He called out in his usual way:

> *"Rapunzel, Rapunzel,*
> *Sweet and fair,*
> *I am here,*
> *Let down your hair."*

Down tumbled the tresses and up climbed the prince. What a shock he had! Instead of his beautiful Rapunzel he found a hideous old crone.

"Your lovebird is here no more," cackled the witch. "She is gone, lost forever. The cat has gotten her and will scratch out your eyes too."

The prince was so distraught that he leaped out of the window, calling out Rapunzel's name.

He landed in the thorny bushes below, which pierced his eyes and made him blind.

For years he roamed around the forest, too miserable to care about the loss of his sight or to try to go back home to his kingdom. He lived on nuts and berries, and at night he slept under the trees with the owls hooting in the branches above him. Then one day he stumbled into a desert.

The sun was blazing and his mind started to wander.

Was that a voice he could hear in the wilderness? Was someone singing? It sounded so much like his beloved Rapunzel. He stood and listened. Yes, it was Rapunzel singing. There she was, in the desert where the witch had left her. He called out to her and they fell into each other's arms. Rapunzel's tears of joy rained down on the prince's eyes and in an instant he could see again, clear as day.

Rapunzel and the prince traveled back to his father's kingdom, where they lived happily, far away from the wicked witch.

Little Mouse
The Story of the Cat

Once there was a scheming old cat who made friends with a mouse. Day after day the wily cat praised the mouse, telling her how neat and tidy she was and what good table manners she had. The mouse enjoyed the cat's compliments, so when the cat suggested they set up house together, she accepted right away.

"The first thing we must do," said the cat as soon as they had settled in, "is to save some food for the winter; otherwise, we shall starve when it starts to snow and there are no scraps to be found on the street. And you, dear mouse, must stop trotting off here, there, and everywhere, or you'll end up in a mousetrap. Then where will I be without my dear little mouse?"

The mouse agreed that they should save some food for the bitter winter, so the two of them pooled

and Lazy Cat
and Mouse in Partnership

all their savings and bought a very large pot of fat.

"Where shall we hide it?" asked the mouse.

"Let's bury it under the altar in the church," replied the cat. "No one ever dares steal anything from there."

So the cat and the mouse buried the precious pot of fat under the altar in the church. Then the mouse set about making their new home all spick-and-span. The cat didn't do any work at all; she just lazed about praising the mouse for her delicious cooking and excellent cleaning. Or else she sat in the sun, her mouth watering at the thought of the delicious pot of fat under the altar.

At long last the cat could bear it no longer: she had to have some of that fat pretty soon or she'd go mad with longing. So one day she said to the mouse, "Would you mind looking after the house by yourself tomorrow? I've

59

just heard from my cousin who's had a new kitten. She's asked me to be the godmother at the christening and I couldn't say no as the baby is brown with white spots."

"Off you go," said the mouse, "and if they have any sweet christening wine, don't forget to bring me some."

Early the next morning the cat went off to the church. There was no christening there, of course; the cat had lied. When no one was looking, she crept behind the altar and dug up the pot. Greedily, she stuck in her paw and licked the fat off her fur. Mmmm, how delicious it tasted. The cat ate more and more and more until she had creamed off the top. Then she put the pot back under the altar and went round the city to see her friends, so she wasn't back home until very late.

"What did they call the baby at the christening?" asked the mouse.

"Top-Off," said the cat, her mind still on the pot of fat.

"What a strange name to give a child," said the mouse.

"It's not half as strange as Crumb Stealer or Cheese Picker, as your nephews are called," said the cat, and went straight to bed.

Barely a week had passed before the cat started longing for more of the creamy fat. So once again she said to the

mouse, "You won't believe this, but my other sister has had a little one too. She's asked me to be the godmother. The new kitten is so pretty, with a white ring around her neck, that I couldn't say no. Could you look after the house while I'm gone tomorrow?"

The mouse agreed and the next day the cat crept off to the church a second time. There she dug up the pot and, before she could stop herself, gobbled up half the fat. Mmmm . . . delicious! When the cat could eat no more, she buried the half-empty pot and set off to see her friends. The moon had risen in the sky when she got home.

"And what did they call this child?" asked the mouse.

"Half-Finished," replied the cat.

"Half-Finished?" said the mouse suspiciously. "I've never heard that name before. I'll bet my tail there's no saint in heaven with that name."

A few days passed and the cat could hardly sleep for thinking about the pot. At last she said to the mouse, "It seems that good things come in threes, for yet another of my sisters has given birth to a kitten. She has also asked me to be the godmother and I can't refuse, as the little one has black fur and white paws."

"Top-Off, Half-Finished," mumbled the mouse.

"They're such odd names, I don't know what to believe."

"You spend too much time on your own," said the cat. "Your head is full of fancies and nonsense. There's nothing to be suspicious of."

"Off you go, then," said the mouse. "I'll clean the house and make the dinner while you're out."

So once again the cat pitter-pattered to the church and dug up the pot under the altar. Again she couldn't help herself and, before you could say "whiskers," the fat was all gone. "That was the best meal I've ever had," purred the cat to herself, and off she went to celebrate with her friends. As before, she did not return home until it was dark and the sky was full of stars.

"And what have they called this child?" asked the mouse straight away.

"All-Gone," said the cat without stopping to think.

"That's the strangest name yet," exclaimed the mouse. "I'm sure you've made it up, although I have no idea why."

Time passed and autumn turned into winter. Soon there was no food to be found outside. The mouse thought of the pot of fat in the church and said to the cat, "Let's go and have some."

"That's a good idea," said the cat.

The two of them set off to the church and dug up the pot. It was, of course, empty.

"I see what's been going on," shrieked the mouse, shaking with rage. "You've been coming here to eat the fat while you were supposed to be at all those christenings. Some friend you are. I should have known not to trust a cat. First Top-Off, then Half-Finished, and finally—"

"Stop it," snarled the cat. "One more word out of you and I'll eat you up."

But it was too late. "All-Gone" had already tripped off the mouse's tongue. Scarcely had she uttered the words when the cat leaped on her and ate her all up. Yum, yum. Sometimes life is not fair at all!

The Princess and

The Story of

One snowy day a queen sat sewing at her palace window. The window frame was made of the finest black ebony, while the snow on the sill glittered white and pure. Suddenly the queen pricked her finger with the needle and three drops of blood fell on the snow. *What a pretty combination that is,* she thought. *Would that I had a child as white as snow, as red as blood, and as black as the ebony of the window frame.*

Nine months passed and sure enough the queen bore the king a little girl. She had skin as white as snow, lips as red as blood, and hair the color of ebony. The queen named her Snow White.

Soon after the baby's birth, the queen passed away. Poor little Snow White had no mother until the day the king married another woman. The new queen was

the Seven Dwarves

Snow White

beautiful but proud and vain, and could not bear to see anyone more lovely than she was. She had a magic mirror, which she kept locked in her bedchamber. Every night she would stand in front of it and ask:

> *"Mirror, mirror, on the wall,*
> *Who's the fairest one of all?"*

And the mirror would always reply:

> *"You, with crowned head and jeweled hand*
> *Have the fairest face in all the land."*

Seven years passed, and Snow White became a kind and beautiful girl. One day the queen went to the mirror and said:

> *"Mirror, mirror, on the wall,*
> *Who's the fairest one of all?"*

And the mirror replied:

   "You, Queen, are beautiful—it's true,

   But Snow White is more beautiful than you."

Then the queen turned purple with rage and envy and, drawing a curtain to hide the mirror, she called for one of her trusted guards.

"Take Snow White into the forest and kill her," she commanded, "and see that you bring me her heart, so that I may know for sure she's dead."

The guard put Snow White in a carriage and took her deep into the forest. But when the time came to kill her, he had not the heart to use his knife. "Run away, my child," he said, "and don't come back to the

palace or else the queen will have you murdered."

Just then a wild boar came crashing through the trees. The guard caught and killed it and later that evening he took the boar's heart to the queen.

"Well done," said the queen, thinking the boar's heart was Snow White's. "You have served me well." And she took the heart and locked it in a little chest.

Meanwhile, Snow White wandered through the forest, looking for somewhere to sleep. The poor child was terrified: All around her, wild animals howled and barked. But none touched her, for they could sense that she had a heart of gold and did not wish them any harm. In the evening she spied a little cottage at the foot of a mountain.

The door was wide open, so she went inside to rest.

Everything in the cottage was surprisingly small. The table was set with seven plates and next to each plate there was a spoon. Beside the spoons there were knives and forks, and seven mugs filled to the brim with wine. By the wall stood seven little beds, each one covered with a white bedspread. Snow White was so hungry and thirsty that she took a sip of wine from every mug and a mouthful of bread and stew from every plate. Then she went to the nearest bed and fell fast asleep.

The owners of the cottage were seven little dwarves who mined the nearby mountains for gold. Soon after Snow White dropped off to sleep, the dwarves returned home to find that someone had been trespassing on their property.

"Someone's been sitting in my chair," said the first dwarf.

"Someone's been eating from my plate," said the second.

"Someone's been nibbling at my bread," said the third.

"Someone's been helping themselves to my stew," said the fourth.

"Someone's been sipping my wine," said the fifth.

"Someone's been using my knife," said the sixth.

"Someone's been sleeping in my bed," cried the seventh. "And she is still here. Come and have a look."

All the dwarves crowded round the bed to look at Snow White.

"What a beautiful child she is," said the eldest. "Let her sleep until the morning." So, quietly, quietly, the dwarves had their dinner and then,

quietly, quietly, they tiptoed to bed. One of them, the smallest, left his lamp close to Snow White so that if she were to wake up during the night, she would not be scared of the dark.

In the morning Snow White opened her eyes and saw the dwarves. At first she was frightened, as she had never seen a dwarf before. But then the youngest brought her a bowl of milk, and the oldest gave her a little cake, and soon she warmed to them and told them all that had happened to her. The dwarves took pity on her and begged her to stay with them. In return Snow White promised to keep house for them; she would clean the cottage, wash their clothes, and prepare a hot supper every night.

Far away, in the palace, the evil queen stood in front of the mirror once more and said:

"Mirror, mirror, on the wall,
Who's the fairest one of all?"

And the mirror replied:

"You, Queen, are beautiful and fair,
But in the cottage, by the hill,
There lives Snow White,
Who's fairer still."

Then the queen knew that she had been tricked and

that Snow White was still alive. Quickly, she painted her face to make it look like an old woman's, put on shabby clothes, and wandered through the forest until she found the dwarves' cottage.

"Good morrow," she said, knocking on the cottage door. "Is anybody here?"

Snow White had been warned by the dwarves that the evil queen might come looking for her, but she did not recognize her stepmother, so cleverly was she disguised. "What are you selling, old woman?" she asked.

"Scarves," replied the evil queen. "Silky scarves in all sizes and colors."

"I'll have one," said Snow White, opening the door to let the queen in.

"You know how to knot a scarf, don't you?" said the queen. "You just wrap it round your neck and pull." And she wound a scarf round Snow White's neck and pulled it so tight that the little girl could not breathe and fell to the floor as if she were dead.

Now I am the most beautiful person in the land, thought the queen as she hurried back to the palace.

In the evening the dwarves returned home and found Snow White lying on the floor. At first they thought she

73

really was dead, but when they noticed the scarf around her neck, they cut it loose and Snow White let out a sigh. Not long afterward she opened her eyes and told the dwarves what had happened.

"The old peddler woman must have been the evil queen in disguise," said the dwarves. "Be careful and don't open the door when we're out, Snow White, or she might fool you again."

Back in the palace, the queen asked the mirror her usual question.

The mirror said:

"You are dazzling, O Queen,

But Snow White

Is the prettiest

There ever has been."

The queen couldn't believe her ears: The wretched child was still alive. "I'll destroy her yet," she fumed, and she fetched her spell book and her potions and made a comb filled with poison. Then, chanting a magic spell, she took the shape of an old crone and ventured back through the forest.

"I am not to let anyone in," said Snow White when she heard knocking at the door.

"I am only here to sell combs," croaked the old crone, poking her head through the window and holding up the poisoned comb. "Surely you are allowed to look?"

Snow White hesitated, then said, "How much does it cost?"

"Try it first," suggested the queen. "Run it through your hair."

Snow White took the comb, and the moment it touched her head, she fell to the ground, poisoned.

"That will teach you to be more beautiful than me," sneered the queen, and she returned once more to the palace.

Later that evening the dwarves came home. When they found poor Snow White on the floor, they gently teased the comb out of her hair. Snow White revived right away.

Meanwhile, the queen hurried to her room and, pulling open the velvet curtain, said:

"Mirror, mirror on the wall,

Who's the fairest one of all?"

The mirror replied:

"You, Queen, are beautiful—it's true,

But Snow White is still fairer than you!"

Now a great rage came over the queen and she

decided to use her most powerful magic against Snow White. She locked herself in the palace dungeons and, summoning all the terrible forces of evil, made an enchanted apple. On one side the magic fruit was good and wholesome, and on the other it was poisonous, so that whoever ate it would die in the greatest pain.

The queen disguised herself as a jolly farmer's wife. Early in the morning she returned to the dwarves' cottage.

"Apples," she chirped. "Nice, juicy apples going fast and going cheap!"

Snow White looked out the window. "I cannot open the door," she said. "The dwarves have forbidden it."

"Surely you can have one of my delicious, juicy apples?" asked the queen.

"No," said Snow White, "I am not to buy anything, not even an apple."

"Are you afraid it might be poisoned?" said the queen. "Look, I'll eat one half and you can have the other." She cut the apple in half and ate the good part. Then Snow White was afraid no more. She took the other half of the apple and held it to her lips. Of course, no sooner had she taken a bite than the poison spread through her body and she fell down dead. "White as snow," roared the queen, "red as blood, black as ebony. No one can save you now!"

She returned to the palace and, standing triumphantly in front of the mirror, said:

> *"Mirror, mirror on the wall,*
>
> *Who's the fairest one of all?"*

And the mirror replied:

> *"You, Queen, are beautiful—it's true.*
>
> *There's no one in the land as fair as you!"*

Then the queen's evil heart was filled with joy, and she drew the curtain over the mirror and slept the sleep of the dead.

Back in the forest, as dusk was falling, the dwarves came home for supper and once again found Snow

White lying on the floor. Gently they lifted her up, washed her face with cold water, and held smelling salts under her nose. But nothing they did could bring Snow White back to life. She was truly dead.

The dwarves laid her on a bier. In the morning they dug a grave for her but, seeing that her cheeks were still red, they said, "We cannot put this child in the dark ground." So they made a glass coffin with Snow White's name written in gold letters on the lid. They placed it on the mountain near the entrance to the mines, so that one of them could always stay beside it to keep the princess company. Snow White lay in the coffin for a long time, but her cheeks never lost their color and her hair remained as shiny and black as ebony.

Then one day a prince came riding over the mountain. He saw Snow White in the glass coffin and she looked so beautiful, so serene, that he could not tear his gaze away from her.

"May I buy the coffin from you?" the prince asked the dwarves.

"Nay," said the dwarves, "we will not part with it for all the money in the world."

"Then let me take her as a gift," begged the prince.

"I shall keep her in my palace, for I cannot bear to live without her."

The dwarves took pity on the poor lad and they let him take Snow White. His servants carried the coffin down the mountain. When they reached the forest, one of them stumbled on a tree root, and with the jolt the piece of poisoned apple popped out of Snow White's mouth. She woke up and, rubbing the sleep from her eyes, said, "Where am I?"

"You are with me," said the prince. "I love you. Will you be my queen and help rule my kingdom?"

Snow White accepted his proposal right away. The prince took her to his kingdom and their wedding was held with much joy and splendor. Among the invited guests was the wicked queen who, while she was dressing for the great feast, could not help standing in front of the mirror once more, for old times' sake. She asked:

> *"Mirror, mirror on the wall,*
> *Who's the fairest one of all?"*

The mirror replied:

> *"You, Queen, are beautiful—it's true,*
> *But the bride is more beautiful than you!"*

82

When the queen heard this, she knew that Snow White had come back to life and that she was the prince's bride. A wild scream escaped her lips. She snatched the mirror from the wall and smashed it to pieces. At the very same moment her heart broke into a thousand fragments too, so that she fell down dead and her evil magic died with her.

After her wedding Snow White went to see the dwarves again. How happy they were to see her alive and well. All seven of them wished Snow White and her prince a long and happy life.

The Swans and the

The Story of

Once upon a time, a king went hunting in a great forest. He was enjoying himself so much that he galloped on ahead, leaving his attendants far behind. Soon he was lost and, try as he might, could not find his way back to his people. He wandered among the trees, getting hungrier and more tired by the minute until, at last, he met an old woman.

"Can you show me the way out of the forest?" he asked her.

"I can help you, indeed," said the woman, who was really a witch, "but only on the condition that you take my daughter as your bride. She is beautiful and clever enough to be your queen."

The king had no choice but to agree, even though he was a widower and had no wish to marry again.

84

Brave Princess

the Six Swans

The witch led him to her hut and introduced him to her daughter. The maiden was truly beautiful, but there was something cold and calculating about her, which made the king very uneasy. Still, the king had given his word that he would marry her, and a king never goes back on a promise.

So he took the maiden by the hand and helped her up onto his horse. The old witch pointed out the way, and before long the king was at the edge of the forest, back with his men. The very next day, he married the witch's maiden and gave her beautiful chambers at the back of the palace.

Now, the king had seven children from his previous marriage—six fine boys and a little girl. He was afraid that his new wife might harm them, so he took them to a castle in the middle of the forest and left them there to be looked after by an old nanny. He came to see them often, but, as the castle was well hidden, he could only find his way to it by using a magic ball of wool. This ball had been given to him by a good fairy; when he threw it on the ground, it unraveled itself along the forest path and showed him the way to his children.

It wasn't long before the new queen noticed that the king went into the forest a great deal. She bribed some of the servants, who told her about the children and how they were hidden in the forest. They told her about the magic ball of wool too, and how it helped the king find the hidden castle. The queen became jealous of the children and determined to get rid of them.

She made seven white shirts. Inside each shirt she sewed a magic charm. When the shirts were finished, she used a magic mirror to find the secret ball of wool and, in no time at all, was galloping on her horse toward the children's hideout.

The children, who were expecting their father, rushed out to meet her. Only the youngest, the little girl, stayed behind in the castle. The queen hugged the boys and kissed them on the cheek; then she gave them the shirts. The boys tried them on, and as soon as the collars were fastened around their necks, they turned into swans and flew off into the sky. Delighted with her work, the wicked queen returned to the palace.

The next day the king came to visit his children. When he found the boys gone and his daughter clutching a handful of swan feathers, he thought that some forest spirit had put a spell on them. But he never for a moment suspected his new wife. Fuming with anger, he told the nanny to pack the girl's clothes, as he wanted to take her back to his palace with him. The little girl was not so keen to meet her stepmother; she begged her father to let her stay in the castle one more night and he agreed.

When the king and the nanny had gone to bed, the girl said to herself, "I must find my brothers," and without any more delay she set out into the forest. She walked and walked until her feet could carry her no longer. Then, quite by chance, she came upon a little hut. She went inside and found six little beds, each one with a cotton pillow. She dared not touch them, so she lay on the floor and went to sleep.

At dusk she was awoken by a rustling sound and six swans came flying in through the open window. They all settled on the floor and started flapping their wings. Their feathers flew off their backs and they turned into boys. The girl realized they were her brothers and was delighted to see them. But the boys said, "You mustn't stay here a moment longer. This is a thieves' lair and if the crooks come back and find you here, they will kill you."

"Then you must look after me," said the girl.

"We can only stay for fifteen minutes," said her brothers. "After that we change into swans again."

"Is there nothing I can do to break the spell?" said the girl.

"No," said the boys, "the task is too hard; we would never ask you to suffer so for us."

"Tell me what to do," begged the girl.

"You must not talk or laugh for six years," said the boys. "And you must make us each a shirt of starwort. If you laugh but once or utter one single word, your efforts will have been in vain and we shall remain swans forever."

"I'll free you," promised their sister. "Come back to me at the end of six years and I'll have the shirts ready."

The brothers nodded and, since the fifteen minutes were up, they turned into swans again. Their sister watched them fly away and then, by the light of the moon, she started looking for starwort. The next morning she began making the shirts.

As the years went by, the girl grew into a young maiden. All alone in the forest she worked at the shirts. Not a word or a sigh passed her lips, and she certainly did not feel like laughing. Never once did she stop stitching.

Now, one day a handsome young prince came hunting in the forest and his servants found the young maiden sitting in a tree.

"Who are you?" they called.

The maiden did not reply but threw down her golden necklace. The servants called the prince and he climbed

up the tree and brought the maiden down in his arms. He asked her who she was in every language he knew, but she never replied nor smiled. Still, the prince could not help noticing how beautiful she was and how well she carried herself. So he took her to his father's kingdom and made her his bride.

The prince's mother did not like the new princess at all. She spoke ill of her at every occasion and said to her friends, "It is very strange that she doesn't speak and that she keeps working away at that starwort. Who knows what evil powers she possesses?"

Some time later the princess had a baby. While she lay sleeping, the prince's mother crept to the cot and stole the child. Then she smeared hare's blood around the princess's mouth and in the morning said: "Look, the witch has devoured her own child."

The prince could not believe that his young wife would do such a thing. But a year later a second baby was born and it too disappeared. When the princess was again found with blood on her lips, his mother said: "Cast her out. She is evil."

"I'll give her one last chance," said the prince.

Soon a third child was born, and it, too, went the way of the others. Now the prince confronted the princess, but she would not say one word in her own defense; she merely continued to stitch her shirts. The judge was called for, and since the princess would not deny that she had killed her own children, she was condemned to burn at the stake.

It so happened that the day the princess was to be burned was also the last day of the six-year silence. The princess had nearly finished sewing the shirts: There was only the sleeve of one missing. When the soldiers came to fetch her, she draped the six shirts over her arm and took them with her to the place of execution. As she stood on the pyre, the swans came flying toward her. She threw the shirts over them, and in an instant they were transformed into young men. Only the sixth brother, who had been given the

unfinished shirt, was not completely changed: One of his arms remained a swan's wing.

The brothers hugged their sister and she turned to the prince and said, "Dearest husband, now that I can speak, I can tell you that I am innocent. Your wicked mother stole our babies and hid them." So it was that the children were found and brought back to their happy parents, while the prince's wicked mother was burned to death instead of the young queen.

The six brothers sent word to their father to tell him that they were all safe and sound. Then they came to live in the palace with their sister, and they spent the rest of their lives in peace and happiness.

Long ago, when wishing could still make dreams come true, there was a king who had many daughters. They were all pretty, but the youngest was so beautiful, she even dazzled the sun.

Sometimes, when the weather was warm, the princess went out in the forest and sat by a cool, deep well. One day she was playing with her favorite golden ball when all of a sudden it slipped out of her hands and sank into the water. The princess tried to fish it out, but it was no use. The well was much too deep.

"Oh dear," said the beautiful princess, and she started to wail and cry.

"What ever is the matter?" croaked a voice behind her.

The princess turned to see a huge frog with a wrinkled neck and bulging eyes. "I have dropped my favorite

Princess and the Frog

the Frog Prince

golden ball in the well," she sniffed. "I'd give anything to get it back. Anything."

"Anything?" echoed the frog, hopping into the water.

"Simply anything," repeated the princess. "I'd give my clothes, my jewels, and even my precious crown. It has twelve diamonds in it."

"I have no use for crowns or jewels," said the frog, "but if you promise to let me come and live with you in your palace, if you say I can eat from your golden plate and sleep on your silken pillow, I'll fetch your ball for you."

What a fool this frog is, thought the princess. *Frogs can only survive near ponds and wells; they can't live with people in houses or palaces.* So she smiled and promised the frog she would take him to the palace with her if he retrieved her ball.

The frog promptly dived down to the bottom of the well, and a minute or two later he surfaced with the golden ball in his mouth.

"Thank you," said the princess. She reached out, took the ball from him, and started running away.

"Wait for me," cried the frog. "Don't you remember your promise?"

But the princess took no heed of his words. She just kept on running and running until she reached her father's palace.

The next day, while the princess was having dinner with her father, something came creeping up the marble stairs, going *plip, plop, plip, plop, plip.* When it reached

the top, there was a knock at the door and a croaky voice called, "Princess, Princess, let me in."

"That must be one of your friends come to visit," said her father the king. "Go and open the door."

The princess did as she was told and, to her horror, she saw the frog sitting on the marble doorstep. *Bang!* The princess slammed the door shut in his face and returned to the table.

"You are trembling," said her father. "Was there a giant out there?"

"No," said the princess, "it was only a frog." And she told her father about the golden ball and how the frog had retrieved it for her.

Just then the frog knocked on the door again. This time he chanted:

"Youngest daughter of the king,

Open up and let me in.

Don't you know what yesterday

You said to me down near the well?

Youngest daughter of the king,

Open up and keep your word."

"A princess should always keep her promise," agreed the king. "Let the frog in and give him some dinner."

So the princess opened the door again and the frog followed her in, along the hall, across the throne room, and into the dining room.

"Lift me up beside you, Princess," he commanded.

Reluctantly, the princess put him on a chair beside her.

"I cannot reach your plate from here," complained the frog. "Put me on the table."

Trying hard not to grimace, the princess put the frog on the table but as far away from her as possible.

"Bring your plate closer, so we can sup together," said the frog. He licked at her food with his tongue and drank milk from her goblet. The princess was so disgusted that she could hardly touch anything. At last the frog said,

"Thank you for that excellent meal. Now take me upstairs to your bed that I might have some sleep."

When the princess heard this, she began to cry. But her father grew angry and said, "You should be grateful to anyone who's helped you in your hour of need. Take the frog up to your room and let him sleep in peace."

The princess picked up the frog with two fingers and, holding him at arm's length, took him up to her bedroom. There she put him down in a corner, hidden behind a pitcher.

The frog said, "It's not fair that you should lie in a warm bed while I have to make do with a cold, stone floor. Let me sleep on your pillow."

Very reluctantly, the princess lifted the frog onto her soft pillow.

"Now give me a kiss," said the frog.

The princess was horrified. "Do not be impertinent," she cried, "or I shall call my guards and ask them to crush you underfoot."

"If you do not kiss me," said the frog, "I shall tell the king. He won't be pleased when I say you have gone back on your word."

Not wanting to get into further trouble with her father,

the princess agreed to kiss the frog. Slowly she bent forward and touched her warm lips to his slimy, cold ones.

All at once, there was a blinding flash of light, and the frog turned into a prince. He was so charming and handsome that the princess was terribly ashamed she'd been so unkind to him and begged his forgiveness. The prince told her how a horrible witch had put a curse on him and how she, the princess, had broken the curse with her kiss.

At dawn a beautiful carriage came to fetch the prince to his kingdom. It was very grand, all made of filigreed gold and drawn by eight strong horses with flowing manes and swishing tails. At the rear stood Faithful Henry, the prince's most loyal servant.

Poor Henry had been very upset when the witch turned his prince into a frog, so the doctor had put three iron bands around his heart to keep it from breaking with sorrow.

The princess asked her father if she might marry the prince, and he consented. So the coach driver cracked his whip and the servants cheered as the coach set off down the street, with Faithful Henry standing in his place at the rear.

When the coach was some distance from the palace, the prince heard a loud crack.

"Henry," he called, "is the carriage falling apart?"

"No, Your Majesty," replied Henry, "it is not the carriage that's breaking, it's one of the iron bands around my heart."

There was another crack, and another. Henry yelled with joy, for at last all three bands had fallen from his heart. Now he was free to celebrate the return of his prince and to take part in the wedding festivities as his master married the beautiful princess.

The Girl Who Spun

The Story of

Once there was a miller who had a beautiful daughter. The man was poor, but he was forever boasting to try and make himself seem important. He lived in a mill, right on the edge of a wood where the king often went hunting. One day the miller happened to meet the king.

"My daughter is so clever," he boasted, "that she can spin ordinary straw into gold."

The king, who loved gold more than anything else in the world, patted the miller on the shoulder. "Send her to my palace tomorrow," he said, "and I'll put her to the test."

So the poor girl had to go to the palace. The king showed her into a little chamber, where there was a big pile of straw and a spinning wheel. "Spin this into gold

106

Straw into Gold

Rumpelstiltskin

by the morning," he said, "or I'll have you put to death."
Then he locked and bolted the door and went away.

"What ever shall I do now?" wondered the girl, and
she started to cry. "No one on earth can turn straw
into gold." Just then the door to the chamber flew
open and a goblin came leaping in.

"Good evening, young lady," he said. "Why are
you crying?"

"I am to spin all this straw into gold by morning,"
said the girl miserably. "But I don't know how."

"What will you give me if I spin the straw into gold?"
asked the goblin.

"My necklace," said the girl.

"Your necklace will do nicely," said the goblin. He sat
down at the wheel and started spinning. *Whirr, whirr,*

whirr—three turns and the bobbin was full of gold thread. The goblin replaced it with another one and—*whirr, whirr, whirr*—three turns and a second bobbin was full of gold. Before long all the straw had vanished and in its place was a neat pile of spun gold. The goblin took the girl's necklace and quickly left the room.

At daybreak the king unlocked the door to the chamber, and when he saw the reels of gold piled neatly on the floor, he was beside himself with joy. "You have done well," he said to the girl. He clapped and his servants brought in a pile of straw TWICE the size of the first one. "Now you must spin this into gold by tomorrow morning,"

he commanded, "or you know what will happen."

He locked and bolted the door once more. The girl sat down and, like the night before, started weeping and howling. But no sooner had the sun set than the door creaked open and there was the goblin again, grinning from ear to ear.

"What will you give me if I spin your straw into gold once more?" he asked.

"I'll give you my ring," answered the girl.

"Your ring will do nicely," said the goblin. He took his place on the stool and—*whirr, whirr, whirr*—the bobbin was soon full of gold thread like the night before. So it

went on till all the straw had been spun into gold.

The king couldn't believe his eyes when he opened the door again at the crack of dawn. He had the girl taken into a bigger room where there was a pile of straw THREE times the size of the first one.

"Spin that into gold," he promised, "and I shall make you my queen. But don't fail me, or you'll lose your head on the chopping block."

When the girl was alone, the goblin came to see her a third time. "What will you give me if I spin the straw into gold yet again?" he asked.

"I have nothing left to give you," said the girl.

"Then promise to give me your first child," said the goblin, "and I'll set to work right away."

The girl thought to herself, *I'm not even married yet— who knows if I shall ever have a child?* And as she was so desperate to save her neck, she promised the goblin her first baby.

The goblin sat at the stool. Once more the spinning wheel turned—*whirr, whirr, whirr*, the spindle bobbed up and down, and before sunrise the straw had been spun into shimmering gold.

In the morning the king kept his word and took the

beautiful miller's daughter as his bride. Time passed and the new queen had a baby. In her happiness she forgot all about the little goblin and the promise she had made to him. But one night the door to her chamber flew open and there stood the little man once more, grinning slyly from ear to ear.

"Now give me what you promised," he said.

The young queen paled and clasped the baby to her chest. "I will give you anything you ask for," she told the goblin, "but, please, I beg you, don't take away my child." And she cried so hard and trembled so violently that at last the goblin took pity on her.

"I shall give you three days' grace," he said. "If you guess my name correctly in that time, I shall let you keep the child."

The queen lay awake all night, trying to remember all the names she had ever heard. In the morning she sent out a messenger to track down all the unusual names he could find. When the goblin arrived, the queen started with the names she knew. But the goblin just shook his head at each and every one of them and said, "That is not my name."

On the second day the queen repeated all the

strange names she had read in the king's library: Loftus, Pimpernel, Fenugreek . . . But once again the goblin shook his head at each and every one of them and said, "That is not my name."

On the third day the messenger returned with exciting news. "Your Highness," he said, "I have not been able to find a new name in two days, but early this morning I came across the hill where the fox bids the hare good night. Right on top of the hill there was a little house, and right in front of the house I saw a log fire burning. Dancing around the fire on one foot was a curious goblin like the one you described. He was laughing and singing:

> *"'Today I bake, tomorrow brew,*
> *Merrily I dance and sing,*
> *For the queen will never find out*
> *My name is RUMPELSTILTSKIN.'"*

When the queen heard the name, she started singing and dancing herself.

As soon as the goblin arrived, she ushered him straight into her chamber and said, "Is your name by any chance Tom?"

"I'm afraid that's not my name," answered the goblin.

"Then could it be Hamish?" asked the queen.

"I'm afraid that's not it either," said the goblin.

"Well, then," said the queen, "is there the slightest chance that it could be RUMPELSTILTSKIN?"

The goblin was furious when he heard his name. "The devil must have told you that," he bellowed, and he stamped his foot so hard that it went right through the floor. He tried in vain to pull it out again; in the end he struggled so hard that he tore himself in two, and died. So the poor miller's daughter who had become queen lived happily ever after with her king and her child.

The Twelve
The Story of the

There was once a king who had twelve beautiful daughters. He was very proud of them and kept a close eye on them all day long. At bedtime he locked them all in one vast bedroom with twelve beds to make sure they were safe. In the morning he unlocked their door himself, with a golden key he kept on a chain around his neck.

One morning when the king unlocked the bedroom door, he saw that the princesses' satin shoes had been danced to pieces. No one knew how the princesses had managed to escape from their room, nor who they had danced with. And they weren't saying, no matter how much their father pleaded with them or scolded them.

The same thing happened the next night and the night after that. The mystery bothered the king, and

116

Dancing Princesses
Shoes That Were Danced to Pieces

when it seemed that the princesses would not stop sneaking out of the palace, he decided to solve it once and for all.

He sent out a proclamation, inviting all the young men of the land to discover the princesses' secret. Anyone who did could choose one of the king's daughters to marry and would inherit the kingdom. But anyone who tried and failed three nights in a row would lose his head on the executioner's block.

Many a dashing young prince accepted the challenge. Each was given a sumptuous supper and at bedtime was shown to a chamber adjoining the princesses' bedroom. The door between the two rooms was kept open, so the prince could observe the king's daughters.

But, in turn, each prince fell asleep at his task and in the morning the princesses' shoes were found tattered and torn. Many princes lost their lives and the princesses' secret remained just that: a secret.

Now, it so happened that a poor soldier found himself on the outskirts of the city where the king lived. He had been wounded in battle and discharged with a medal, but he had no idea where he was to settle or how he was going to earn a living. By chance he met a kind old woman who, seeing the pain and weariness in his face, said, "Where are you going, my son?"

And he replied jokingly, "I have no idea, but I might try and discover where the king's daughters dance at night, and then I could become king."

"In that case," said the woman, who was really a kind witch, "do not drink the wine that the princesses offer you, because it will have a sleeping potion in it. Just pretend to be fast asleep, and when the princesses go out, follow them closely." She handed the soldier a cloak. "Put this on your shoulders," she whispered, "and it will make you invisible; that way you can observe the girls without being seen yourself."

118

The soldier thanked the old woman and hurried to the palace. Even though he looked poor, he was as well-received as the princes had been. He was given a delicious supper and shown to the room adjoining the princesses' chamber. As he was about to get into bed, the eldest offered him a goblet of wine. The soldier pretended to drink it, but when the girl wasn't looking, he emptied the goblet into the chamber pot under the bed. Then he lay down, yawned, and began to snore loudly.

"The fool is asleep

already," said the eldest princess. "The journey to the palace must have tired him out."

"Poor wretch," said another. "He is sure to lose his head in three days' time."

Then the twelve princesses put on silk party dresses, jeweled crowns, and satin dancing shoes. Just before leaving, they took one last look at the soldier to make sure he was still fast asleep.

"Are you certain he will not wake up before the morning?" asked the youngest princess. "I have an awful feeling that something dreadful is about to happen."

"You are always in dread of one thing or another," mocked the eldest. "There is nothing to fear." Then she knocked on one of the beds and it sank into the floor, revealing a secret staircase. The princesses descended through the opening, one after another.

The soldier, who had secretly been watching everything from his bed, put on his magic cloak and quickly followed them. It was dark in the passage, and halfway down the stairs he stepped on the youngest princess's gown.

"We're being followed," cried the princess. "Someone has just tugged on my gown."

"Don't be foolish," said the eldest sister. "You must have caught your dress on a nail."

At the bottom of the stairs was a garden full of silvery trees, which shone brightly and filled the place with light. The soldier, unable to help himself, reached out and snapped off a twig.

"Did none of you hear that noise?" said the youngest princess. "I am sure we are not alone."

"It is only our princes who wait for us," scolded the eldest princess. She led the way into a second garden, where the trees were made of gold, and then on to a

third, where the trees were laden with diamonds.

In each garden the soldier broke off a twig and the youngest princess gasped at the sound, but she did not say anything else to her sisters for fear of being ridiculed.

At last the princesses reached the shores of a lake. The soldier, coming up behind them, saw twelve handsome princes, each one sitting in a boat with a golden lion's head on the prow. Every princess got into a boat, and the soldier—fearing he might be left behind—hopped in with the youngest.

"The boat seems very heavy tonight," said her prince as he rowed.

"It must be the summer heat," said the youngest princess. "I feel a bit tired and listless too."

Soon all twelve boats were moored outside a palace on the other side of the lake. Each prince took his princess by the hand and led her up a flight of marble steps into a beautiful ballroom. There the happy couples danced to the sound of music, the princesses whirling gaily around in their satin shoes. The soldier danced too, and every time he brushed past the youngest princess, she would stifle a gasp and say, "I can feel a presence in this room; I am sure of it."

123

By three o'clock the princesses' shoes were worn to shreds. It was time for them to leave, and their princes rowed them back across the lake. This time the soldier sat next to the eldest princess and she did not notice his presence, because she was so tired and sleepy.

When they got to the secret passage, the soldier hurried on ahead and jumped back into bed. The princesses, peeping into his room, heard him snoring and assumed that he had been asleep all the time they were gone.

The next night the soldier followed the princesses again. Everything happened as before and the princesses danced until their shoes were worn to pieces. On the third night the soldier stole a wine goblet from the food table in the ballroom, which he hid under his cloak.

At last it was time for the soldier to be summoned before the king. "Have you solved the mystery yet?" asked the king. "Where do my daughters go at night? And who do they dance with?"

"I have solved the mystery, Your Majesty," replied the soldier. "Your daughters escape through a secret tunnel to a palace on the shores of an underground lake. There

126

they dance with twelve handsome princes who row their boats across the water to fetch them."

He showed the king the silver, gold, and diamond twigs and gave him the wine goblet. The king called for the princesses at once and, seeing the evidence in the soldier's hands, they confessed all.

So the king asked the soldier to choose one of the princesses as his bride, and he took the eldest, because she had a mischievous smile and was the closest to him in age. The wedding was held that very same day with much feasting, singing, and, needless to say, dancing. Everyone at the party danced until their shoes had fallen to pieces.

The End